SMOKED

A Snack-Sized Mystery

SMOKED

A Snack-Sized Mystery

Jeff Schmoyer

Jmars Ink

Art by Ani Sledgianowski
Back cover smoke effect by Corina Rainer, Unsplash

Published by Jmars Ink
Visit JmarsInk.com

ISBN 979-8-9881866-0-1

Acknowledgments

A feast of thanks to my fabulous beta readers
Deborah L Brewer, MB Partlow, Shannon Smithwick,
and Robert Spiller.

Chapter One

Matt used his butt to push open the screen door to the backyard of the Rusty Pig. He backed outside while carefully balancing two sheet pans piled high with heavily-seasoned, raw chicken and pig parts.

His waitress sat on one of the picnic tables near the blackened steel smoker, a big grin on her face. "I don't know what you've got in there, but you've outdone yourself."

"Are you screwing with me, Katie? I haven't put anything into the smoker yet."

She held out a wad of smoked meat. "Try some."

"Don't tell me somebody has messed with Old Betsy. I knew I should get a lock for her. We have that food blogger coming this afternoon—everything needs to be perfect or we're out of business."

Matt dropped the sheet pans onto a picnic table and yanked the door handle of the smoker. The low angle of the early morning sun made it difficult to see into the darkness. He reached inside and pulled out a charred trucker's hat. "What the...?"

He turned and saw Katie crumple onto the dew-laden grass.

Chapter Two

In my many years as a food critic, no one has ever tried to serve me people. I've traveled around the world and have been fed every part of every critter you can think of, sometimes for cultural reasons, and sometimes because the chef had to make his mark. That mark has left me on my knees in front of the porcelain on more than one occasion.

I've been told the fur I'm eating flosses my teeth while I chew. I've been told that it is supposed to be that color, never mind that the color exists nowhere in the natural world. I've been fed flakes of gold, though it adds no flavor or texture to the dish. I've spent time after the meal trying to figure out how I could recover the gold and save up for a boat.

But never ever have I been fed a person. I've heard what it tastes like, and knew I swallowed bits of myself every day. I've probably eaten far more exotic creatures than ordinary human. But still, I had no desire to join the ranks of cannibal.

I looked over the chain link fence, decorated with yellow police tape, and watched as chains were wrapped around the big, black smoker, and it was hoisted onto a flatbed truck. A police detective—at least I hoped that was what he was, seeing he had a gun strapped under one arm—finished talking to the cook. As the cop walked away, a man in an expensive-looking suit put his arm around the cook and dragged him into the building.

I've come across a surprising number of dead bodies in service of my chosen vocation—some deaths by natural causes—the bad timing of having a heart attack at the teppan table for birthday dinner with the family, for example. Other deaths have had more sinister origins. Given my flexible schedule and general nosiness, I've been able to help solve a murder or two.

As I walked off to find someplace else to eat lunch, I wondered if the morgue in this small town was big enough to handle the outsized smoker.

Chapter Three

The police detective jogged down the stairs to meet with the medical examiner. He found Lou at his desk, in a staring match with a sandwich.

"Pulled pork was a bad choice for lunch today, Joe," said the ME.

Joe sniffed the medicinal odor of the room. "Is it ever a good choice around here? What can you tell me about the victim, Lou?"

"Not much more than you already know—adult, male, no clothing other than the hat you brought in, so no ID. Fingerprints are a bit of a challenge. I can tell you there was plenty of smoke in his lungs."

"So he wasn't dead when someone put him into the smoker."

"Or when he crawled in," Lou countered.

"Are you saying he did this to himself?" Joe wasn't buying it.

"I'm saying I haven't found any discernible trauma to the body other than what is to be expected under the circumstances. And, of course, that chunk removed from his hindquarters post-mortem. Perhaps he was looking for a warm place to sleep one off."

"Alright, let me know when you get more. You gonna eat that sandwich?"

"Take it."

Chapter Four

I stared blankly at the menu for the Seaside Bistro, reflecting on the irony of the name as the place must have been a thousand miles from any ocean and was more of a dump than any bistro I had ever been in. Dusty plastic fish, crabs, and lobsters dotted the walls. In front of the back partition, a cracked, empty fish tank stored what looked like broken cash register parts and old credit card machines. Perched on the partition was a taxidermied seagull.

Truly a delightful place to enjoy a meal.

I felt a pair of eyes focus on me and I looked up. "Matt, thank you for meeting me." I motioned for him to take the other chair at the two-top.

"I'm sorry you had to come all this way and now you can't try out the Rusty Pig," Matt said as he sat down.

"Don't worry about it, kid. When I plan a road trip, I visit several places along the way. Believe me, this isn't the first time I've arrived at a bar, diner, food truck, or what have you and found it locked up for good."

A gentleman—I gave him the benefit of the doubt—in a dirty apron soon stood at the side of our table. He looked disdainfully at Matt. "What are you doing here?"

"A guy's gotta eat," Matt said.

"Oh, that's right," the man said, "your dive was closed by the county. You seem to have misunderstood what it means to serve your customers. Or maybe you cooked that ridiculous food blogger. Was he going to give you a bad review?"

Matt shot daggers at the man in the dirty apron. I saw on Matt's face that he might be capable of murder.

"Who's this?" the man continued.

I thrust out my hand. "I'm the ridiculous food blogger. My friends call me Murph. You can call me Mr. Murphy."

The man took a step back and I wondered if he was about to make a break for the kitchen.

Truth be told, my food blog was a bit ridiculous, starting with the name—Murphy Slaw. I enjoyed food, and I liked others to enjoy it with me. It's said that some people eat to live and some people live to eat—I live to talk about eating.

The man finally composed himself and grabbed my hand. "I'm Sam Stain." He made a wide sweep with his arms, "Mine."

"Nice place you've got here," I lied.

He snatched the menu off the table. "You won't need this. I'll show you what real barbeque is all about."

"But isn't this a seafood place?" I had been in too many establishments where they thought they could be everything to everyone. In my experience, you should go experience a different restaurant.

Sam acted like he didn't hear me and strode off. I finally had a chance to talk turkey with Matt. "When are you getting a new smoker and reopening? I'm looking forward to tasting what I heard is the best barbeque in these parts."

"I don't know if we will be able to reopen. We weren't exactly making bank, and a new smoker the size of Old Betsy can be pricey."

Old Betsy—I liked a man who cared enough to name his cooker.

"I heard you had lines out the door. How big a place is the Rusty Pig?"

"There are a couple of two-tops and a couple of four-tops inside."

"And I saw half a dozen picnic tables out back," I added. "I checked out your menu online, and the prices look reasonable. If people line up for your food, I'm not sure why you're not making decent dough."

"I don't know either, but the bank account is always about to head south of zero."

Restaurants are probably the toughest businesses to keep going. Even with big crowds and good reviews, some of the best joints I've visited have gone the way of the dodo. But one cook/owner and one waitress, a tiny building and an old rusted smoker—how bad could the overhead be?

Changing the subject, I asked, "Any idea who got smoked last night?"

"No idea." Matt quickly looked to the front door. I was getting the feeling that no one wanted my company today.

Before I could wheedle any more from Matt, Sam showed up with several plates of starters. I've found that when a restaurant tried to overwhelm me with the sheer number of dishes, it meant that they hoped I could find at least one I would give a positive review. Many times that was not the case.

First up—a single pork rib. It was cut so close to the bone that there was no meat to taste so I moved on. Next up—actual seafood at a place that claimed to be a seafood house—a single sea scallop. For the uninitiated, those are the big ones. This scallop looked a bit odd, though. It was fairly flat—not thick like you might normally see. It was also denser than it should be. A scallop should have a grain like a good steak. Something was off with the taste as well. I suspected fraud.

Finally, there was something that looked like lumpy pudding. I gave it a sniff and wished I hadn't. It could have been some kind of chowder, but it was room temperature for who knows how long. I took a hard pass and set it out of reach, saving Matt from this putrid-smelling app.

Mind you, none of this food came with any kind of description. Sam had simply dropped the plates and whizzed off to the kitchen, presumably to scare up the mains.

Once the first course was dealt with, I turned back to Matt. "I understand your waitress had an unfortunate experience this morning. How is she doing?"

"Katie? She took off before the cops showed up. Her mom says she's locked herself in her bedroom and won't talk to anybody."

"It must have been quite a shock when she found out what she had eaten."

"Shock doesn't begin to..." Matt clammed up. It was obvious he knew more than he wanted to tell me.

Before I could pry further, Sam was back with several more plates. It was too bad we were the only customers in the joint, and he didn't have anybody else to occupy some of his time and cooking…uh…skills. I asked him to stick around and tell me what was on each plate this time.

Sam pointed out the grilled Chilean sea bass—he served a healthy portion, I might add. Next up was baked halibut, followed by the acclaimed barbeque.

"This is the best brisket you'll ever eat," Sam overpromised as he glared at Matt.

"And this last dish," I asked.

"Surely I don't need to explain fish and chips to you."

"I would like to know what kind of fish is lurking beneath the breading."

"It's cod, of course. What else would it be?"

"I've found that salmon makes a flavorful substitute," I replied.

Sam grumbled his way back to the kitchen.

Matt and I started with the brisket—I wanted his expert opinion. "What do you think?"

"No smoke. It's a decent piece of meat, but it's made in the oven. Don't know how he can call it barbeque," Matt said.

"Yeah, it's still better than I expected from this place."

On to the trio of fishes. I started by prying some of the breading from the fried cod so I could actually taste the fish. It wasn't as flaky and light as good cod should be, if it was even cod at all.

"Do you eat much seafood, Matt?"

"Here? No."

"Try the sea bass. It's usually one of my favorite fish."

Matt took a forkful. "It's okay, I guess. It doesn't really taste like much."

I stabbed some and gave it a try. "You're right." I dug into the halibut. "Does this taste the same to you?"

He forked a piece. "Yeah, they all seem the same to me, but I'm not a foodie like you."

I took that as a compliment. In my pseudo-expert opinion, they did all seem the same, just prepared differently.

Something fishy was up.

Worst of all, the brisket had been the most passable dish at a seafood place—I missed my own baked salmon.

I wasn't able to get Matt to say any more about the morning events at the Rusty Pig. I couldn't tell whether he was protecting himself, Katie, or someone else. In any case, it was no use trying to get anything further from him.

"You should probably take off before Sam presents you with the bill for all this food," I said. "He won't dare give me one and risk a bad review."

I made it a policy to pay for all the meals I critiqued. There was no need for it to look like I could be bought. A great meal at a fair price was bribery enough for me. As for this meal, no review or payment would be forthcoming.

Matt happily bolted for the door just as Sam appeared with, hopefully, one final course. It was a dessert plate with samples of his many store-bought treats, all bathing in a pool of melted ice cream. Among the haphazardly arranged Ho Hos and Ding Dongs was a stroopwafel—I liked those caramel-filled wafers. Sam hadn't removed its wrapper, saving it from the vanilla-flavored soup. I wiped it off with my napkin and pocketed it.

I was finally left alone to contemplate what had transpired today. Who would murder and smoke someone? I already knew of three possibilities. There was Matt, of course. His waitress, too. They both had access to the smoker. But I didn't have any idea of what their motives might be. Then there was Sam. His motive was clear—shut down the competition. The Seaside Bistro would fare far better without a good restaurant down the street.

But I needed to know more. Perhaps Katie would be willing to talk to me.

Chapter Five

I knocked on the front door of a tidy little house not far from the Rusty Pig. A petite woman who looked as sweet as crème brûlée soon stood before me.

"Mrs. Miller, I'm Murph Murphy. Would you mind if I had a chat with Katie?" I asked.

"Are you a cop?" Her eyes narrowed and she looked me up and down.

So much for sweet.

"No, I'm a bit of a food enthusiast, and I thought I might be able to help."

"Why would she need a food nerd?"

It seemed her daughter had told her nothing of her morning meal—something I would not correct.

Mrs. Miller threw the door wide open. "Down the hall on the right. Good luck."

I knocked gently on the bedroom door. "Katie? My name is Murph. Can we talk?"

"Are you a cop?"

What was it with this family? Were they secret rum runners?

"No, I'm a food blogger. I was hoping we could talk about the Rusty Pig."

The door opened a crack, just enough for me to see a young lady with curly blonde hair and red eyes.

"Then you probably want to talk to Matt. I'm just a waitress," she said.

"I know. I spoke to Matt. He said you had quite the morning."

She pulled the door open further and went to sit on the bed.

I stepped inside and pushed the door most of the way closed. No need for her mother to overhear our conversation.

"I really can't talk about what happened," Katie said.

I could understand that. "Tell me about Matt, then."

"He's always super nice to me. He told me to take off as much time as I needed."

"Matt said this could be the end of the Rusty Pig. There might be no place for you to go back to."

She sniffled. "I hope that's not true. This is the best job I've ever had. Matt might not be so good with money, but he's a great cook, or chef even."

"Has he had formal training?"

"I don't think so. He was the cook at his father's diner till his dad got sick and passed away. The stress of his father's death and the responsibility of running the whole restaurant were too much for him, and it closed. If he didn't have a partner at the Pig, I'm sure it would be history, too."

"I didn't know there was a partner."

"Well, he's kind of a silent partner. I don't know much about him, just that he takes care of the business, like collecting the money and paying the bills. Matt is happy to just cook and chat up the customers."

It was time for me to go there. "I'm sure it must've been quite traumatic when you found out what you'd eaten this morning. I've eaten so many different animals that I've lost track. I thought talking about it might help."

She started bawling louder than my second wife on our wedding night.

"I ate my boyfriend," she cried.

Wait, what?

"Your boyfriend? How do you know?"

"His hat—it was in Old Betsy."

It was one thing to find out you had mistakenly eaten someone. It must be something else entirely to find you'd eaten someone you knew, and possibly loved.

"Are you sure it was his hat?"

Her sobbing started to ease. "He wore it everywhere. He was a truck driver and that was his uniform."

Matt had lied to me about not knowing who the victim was. What else might he have been lying about?

"Do you know anyone who might have wanted to hurt your boyfriend?"

"No, Jeremy Jenks was a good guy. I was lucky to have him." She suddenly put one hand on her stomach and the other over her mouth and ran out of the room.

I wasn't sure how I might help now, given this unexpected twist. I let myself out and pondered my next move. Perhaps a visit to the police would be enlightening.

Chapter Six

I rolled up to the front desk of the police station like a boss. "I'd like to talk to the detective working the Rusty Pig case."

"Can I tell him why?" asked the officer behind the desk.

"I have some information that could be pertinent to the case." That should get me an audience with someone who has some answers.

"Just a moment." He disappeared into the back, then quickly returned and ushered me into an office. Sitting at the desk in front of me was the detective I had seen earlier in the day, gun still strapped under his arm. The nameplate on the desk read "Det. Joe," followed by a bunch of letters I didn't have time to unscramble.

"You are?" the detective inquired.

"I'm Murphy." I put out my hand but found no takers.

"Have a seat, Mr. Murphy. I saw you at the crime scene this morning."

How observant of him.

"I'm a food critic. I came to review the Rusty Pig but found I didn't care for the special of the day."

"I'm sure you've heard that criminals often return to the scene of the crime. Where were you last night?"

The guy got right down to business.

"I was driving in from Denver."

"Anyone vouch for that?"

I hadn't thought that I might need an alibi. "You could talk to Irma, but I don't know that you'll get much out of her."

"Irma?"

"Irma is my car. She was with me the whole time."

Detective Joe stood up and walked around his desk to tower over me. He looked to be in great shape—the exact opposite of me.

"I don't find murder funny," he said.

This meeting was not going at all the way I'd planned.

Detective Joe walked back around to his chair and sat down. "You said you had information."

"I think your victim is Jeremy Jenks."

"The waitress' boyfriend?"

I thought he hadn't interviewed Katie. "How did you know that?" I asked.

"I'm a detective. So, you say you weren't in town, but you know who the victim is." He wrote down some notes on a pad on his desk.

If I wasn't on his suspect list before, I was now. "I don't know Jeremy. I talked to the waitress and she thinks it was him."

"It could be Jenks, or someone else," he said.

"But the hat Katie told me about belonged to him, didn't it?" I wasn't ready to surrender.

"It could be his hat, and he could have lost it when he put the body into the smoker."

Good point. I hadn't thought of that.

He continued, "We're trying to contact Mr. Jenks but haven't gotten ahold of him yet. He could be on the road for a job, or hiding out, or maybe he's in our morgue."

"I can't be your only suspect. What about Matt or Katie?"

"We are looking into both Mr. Rio and Miss Miller."

"Did they have alibis? Is there anyone else you know who might have done it?" I still wanted to come away from this apparent suicide mission with some new information.

"Mr. Murphy, if you aren't involved, what is your interest in my case?"

"Troubleshooting is kind of a hobby of mine, and murder is the worst kind of trouble."

"Perhaps it's time you found another hobby—or maybe stick to food."

"Food has gone way beyond being a hobby. It's my job or my life or something."

Before we could continue our banter, there was a sharp knock at the door. Without waiting for so much as a "Who is it?" or "Come in," the door flew open and a gentleman in a lab coat burst in.

"Sorry, Joe. Didn't know you had company," the new arrival said.

"It's alright, Lou. Mr. Murphy was leaving. We're done here, right, Mr. Murphy?"

"There is one more thing, but it can wait while you two talk." I quickly stepped out of the room and found a chair right next to the door to marinate myself in. The door shut but then popped back open just enough so I could hear it all. I looked to ensure the desk officer couldn't see me and quietly leaned toward the gap.

"What's the rush?" the detective asked his new guest.

"I got the lab report back on the Rusty Pig case. The vic's stomach contained alcohol and Rohypnol—enough to make him really pliable, but not kill him. Death was caused by asphyxiation from the smoke. I'm ruling it a homicide."

"I thought as much. Any updates on who he is?"

"The state takes forever to process the DNA. I'll tell them we've upgraded it from suspicious death to homicide and see if they'll speed it up."

I heard who I now knew was the medical examiner come toward the door, and I sat up straight. I grabbed the newspaper from the chair next to me and pretended to look otherwise occupied. *Great news—the paper said coffee was good for you again.*

The door opened.

"Thanks for coming up, Lou," said the detective.

"Sorry again for interrupting." The ME offered me an apologetic glance as he headed toward the stairs.

I stood to face the detective.

He said, "You said there was something else, Mr. Murphy?"

Something else. Something else.

"Where can a guy get a decent cup of coffee in this town?" I stammered.

"Try the bakery on Main. Have a donut for me. See, I can be funny."

"Um…sure."

"Goodbye, Mr. Murphy. Oh, and don't leave town. Not until I speak to Irma."

Now that was funny.

"But seriously, stay put." He stepped back and closed his office door.

Nuts. I had another restaurant to review that night—and it wasn't in town.

Chapter Seven

Since evidently I wasn't going anywhere, I figured I'd check out the bakery on Main—"The Apple Bakery," the sign out front read. I hoped they had something better than a donut.

They did. The case was stocked with all manner of goodies, and the baker was still at work at the marble. Usually a baker worked the wee hours of the morning, and all the good stuff was long gone by noon.

As I stood feasting my eyes on everything from blueberry muffins to turnovers, the baker wiped off her hands and joined me at the bakery case.

"What would you like?" she asked.

"I heard the coffee here is good. And I like everything I see." I had eaten a lot of baked goods in my life, and I wasn't about to stop then.

"Sorry, I can't give you everything. We're expecting a large turnout tonight."

Did she not realize I was joking, or was she being cute? "Then what do you recommend?"

"The peach tarts are a favorite."

We weren't off to a good start as peaches weren't in season. I tried a different tack. "How about something chocolate?"

"Chocolate orange croissant?" she offered.

Now we were talking. Chocolate and orange was one of my favorite combinations. If she had sprinkled in some cardamom, I might have changed my current stance on marriage. "Yes, please."

She put my croissant onto a plate, set it on the counter by the cash register, and walked to the coffee machine.

I called over to her, "What's happening here tonight?" If the pastry tasted as good as this place smelled, I could make a return visit.

"There's a big All or Nothing tournament."

I had never heard of it. "Is that like Truth or Dare?"

"No, it's a card game. You can come watch, or even try your hand at it."

Was she flirting with me? Did she just invite me back later? "Will I see you here?"

"Heavens no. I'll be long asleep by then so I can get baking by 3 a.m."

That's right—she was the baker. And I had a terrible time reading women. My ex-wives would agree.

I collected my coffee and pastry and went to sit on a stool at the long bar top facing the window. I looked out at the street and took a sip of my steaming drink. The detective was right— not bad at all.

I spun my plate of promise to find the best angle for the requisite photo—if there was no picture, I didn't eat it. Food blog business out of the way, I picked up my treat. *Ooh, it was still a little warm.* The smell of orange wafted upward. The puff pastry melted in my mouth. One bite and I was transported to a Parisian sidewalk café.

I tried to stay in the moment but other thoughts intruded. Perhaps it wasn't Jeremy in the cooker. If not, he certainly should be added to my list of suspects. But there was that whole motive thing, and I didn't have anything to go on. It might be a while before Katie was coherent enough for further interrogation, but there's a good chance Matt would know him.

Before I could come up with an excuse to call Matt, a flashily-dressed woman rushed in from the front door.

"You're that guy!" she announced.

"Well, I am a guy," I responded.

"That food guy!"

"Oh, yes, I am that guy. Care to sit?" I hadn't really needed to offer as she had already placed her large purse onto the bar—almost spilling my coffee—and slid onto the stool next to mine.

This wasn't all that unusual. Though I didn't have my own TV show, my picture and food blog videos were plastered all over the Internet so I did get recognized once in a while. It was one reason I didn't try to do secret reviews of restaurants. I let them know I was coming so they could put on their best face, if they so chose.

"I'm Murph."

She said, "I know! I know everything about you."

Hmm. She might have been more stalker than fan.

She stuck out her hand. "Kimberly Wilson. Everybody calls me Kimber 'cause I'm a real pistol."

I didn't get the reference. I shook her hand for far too long as I couldn't get her to let go of mine. As she finally released me, I saw her purse move and a wet nose emerge from the open end.

"A rat!" I immediately regretted shouting that in an eatery, but it was not the worst thing I had ever done. And the baker seemed to be out of earshot.

Kimber reached into her bag and pulled out the hairy beast. She held its face tightly against hers. "Murphy's not a rat—he's my sweet boy."

Murphy—seriously?

He twitched his nose in the direction of my treat. "You are cute, but I'm not sharing my croissant."

Kimber said, "That's okay. I had a snack earlier."

"No, I was talking to…" Maybe I could turn this off-the-rails encounter to my advantage and get some food tips from a local. "Do you both come here often?" Cliché, I knew.

"Oh, no, we're visitors, like you. I'm staying at the Open Arms. Is that where you're staying?"

"Yes," I squeaked. My stalker knew where I lived.

"Great! Then I'll see you at breakfast." With that, she stuffed Murphy back into her purse and flew out the door.

Ah, the morning's continental breakfast at the Open Arms—I expected no one in charge of it had ever been to the continent. The entire selection was cereal and toast—bread, actually, as the toaster was broken. And, of course, the lukewarm brownish water they called coffee. I didn't need much of an excuse to blow off their free breakfast the next morning for the goodness that was The Apple, and Kimber had given it to me.

With my new…um…friend gone, I could finally spend more quality time with my snack and try to come up with an excuse to talk to Matt again. *Bingo.* I hit redial on my phone.

"Hi Matt, Murph. Do you have time to meet up again? I'd like to try to help you find some money for a new smoker. Great! See you at the Pig in a bit."

Chapter Eight

I took a leisurely stroll to the Rusty Pig—had to work off my buttery indulgence somehow. Matt met me on the front porch and we sat down in a couple of plastic chairs. On a side table between us were two glasses of lemonade. Matt picked them both up and offered one to me.

I hesitated. I didn't want to take the drink from him and banish the flavors of chocolate and orange still lingering on my palate—or perhaps, as Matt could be a murderer, it was self-preservation. But I was trained to be polite and took a slurp—well maybe not all that polite. The lemonade was tart and not overly sweet with a hint of...*what was it?* There was also a bit of heat to the finish. I looked into the glass.

"I taste strawberry but I don't see any. Am I crazy?" There was a question I should never ask anybody.

"The secret is to chop up frozen strawberries, then bundle them in cheesecloth and float it in the lemonade pitcher while it chills. It keeps the strawberry pulp and seeds from clogging up a straw. I usually add a crushed sprig of mint to the packet, but we're out of it right now so I tossed in a couple of jalapeño coins."

Neat trick. Maybe this kid was a chef.

"Tell me about yourself," I said.

"I was raised in a diner. My dad was the chief cook and bottle washer, and the staff was my babysitter. When my dad passed, I tried to make a go of it, but the landlord kept raising the rent and I couldn't keep up with the bills. Most of the staff drifted away, and I had to close it. Katie had just started working there when I locked the door for the last time."

"High overhead will kill you."

"While I was still grieving my losses— well, more like feeling sorry for myself—my aunt passed. She was the last of my family."

This kid couldn't catch a break.

"She left me this place." He motioned to the front door. "It had been vacant for years. Katie helped me clean it up and get it open."

"And the name—where did that come from?"

"On the front of the old converted house were just the three letters 'BBQ.' It was always referred to as the old barbeque joint. I don't think I ever heard another name for it. While we were cleaning up, I found a large steel cutout of a pig behind the stove. I hung it out front and people started calling the place the Rusty Pig even before we opened."

I needed a picture of that hog for the blog, but there were other priorities. "Let's talk about how to get you a new smoker and get your doors back open. How's your cash position?"

"Cash? What's that?"

He sounded like he wasn't kidding.

"How about if we take a look at your books and see what's up?"

"If you think it will help, come on inside. They're on the same computer we use for the register."

I snapped a picture of the steel pig sign and followed Matt through the doorway. We pulled a couple of stools up to the counter and Matt entered the password into the computer.

"I don't use this for much besides putting in food orders," he said.

"No problem. I can take it from here, if you don't mind." I had poked at lots of restaurant computers, what with my troubleshooting hobby.

I called up one of the reports. "This is your profit and loss statement. It's probably the most important thing for you to keep track of. If you look at the income section here at the top, you can see that you are actually pulling in an okay amount of money for a business your size, though I would have expected more from the traffic you tell me you get. The expense section below shows you are also spending almost every penny of that income."

"Isn't that good?"

"Well, no. The difference between income and expenses is called profit or loss. You need profit to do things like buy a new smoker."

"So I don't have profit?"

"None to speak of. Let's drill down into the expenses and see if we can find out where all the money is going." I clicked here and there for a bit and finally had a report of the monthly outgoing cash. There was all the usual stuff you'd expect for a food service business—food, utilities, payroll.

I stopped at that last one. "There seem to be three paychecks every two weeks. Do you have another employee?"

"That's probably for Ham."

"Ham? You pay your pigs?" I couldn't resist.

"No, he's my business partner, Hampton Collins."

Ah, the mysterious business partner. "What can you tell me about this Ham fellow?"

"He owns businesses and real estate all over the area. He said he would handle all the business stuff that I can't seem to get right, and I could just take care of the day-to-day. I really needed the help, so we opened the Pig together.

Since then, he's pretty much stayed behind the scenes."

"Did you know he was getting a paycheck?"

"Not really. But I guess he needs to make money off the Pig somehow."

I looked back at the screen. "There is an expense labeled 'Rent' every month. Didn't you tell me your aunt left you this place free and clear?"

"She did. Maybe it's a mistake."

I checked each expense item more closely and found "mistake" after "mistake." Somebody was up to no good, and Matt didn't seem to know enough for it to be him. But then again, this could all be an act. Maybe he had decided it was time to shut down the Rusty Pig before an audit showed the fraud. Still, you could close up a business without murdering someone and getting the county to do it for you. And why now? It didn't add up—just like the books.

It was getting late and I still had a dinner to get to. But there was one more topic I wanted to broach.

"I visited Katie," I said.

"How is she?"

"She's not all that great, but I suspect you already know that."

He crossed his arms but didn't speak.

"She told me about Jeremy."

That was all it took to get Matt going. "That jerk has ruined my business. He wasn't the nice guy that Katie thought he was. I'm glad he's out of her life for good."

That sounded a little like a confession. "I take it you weren't best friends."

"He was the delivery guy for some of our supplies, like the cornmeal for the hush puppies. That's how he met Katie." Matt slowed. "They had a big fight yesterday—a real blowout. And now he's dead. And you know what happened next. Katie must be in a real bad place."

So Katie and Jeremy had a big fight. That could be motive. She could be faking being upset, hiding out in her bedroom till the heat cooled.

"Yeah, it could take some time for her to get over this," I said.

"Oh." Matt deflated. "Then she won't be coming back to work?"

"You like her, don't you, Matt?"

"Of course I like her. She's the best employee I've ever had, and the customers love her."

It seemed like the customers weren't the only ones who loved her. So there was another motive for Matt. Boy loved girl. Girl had mean boyfriend. Boy stuffed girl's boyfriend into a smoker. I was sure I had seen this played out a thousand times before.

I had to get ready for dinner so I bid Matt adieu and headed out to find wherever Irma had gotten to.

Chapter Nine

It was getting dark as Irma and I took the drive to the next town. We drove very carefully as being pulled over leaving the town I was told not to leave seemed like a bad idea.

Along the way, I reviewed the suspect list with Irma. I told her about Matt, Katie, Jeremy—who may or may not be the victim—and a new addition, Matt's partner, Ham. I didn't mention that I was also a suspect, as I didn't want Irma to think less of me.

We arrived at a place simply named "Steak."

"Table for one," I said to the hostess.

She shrugged her shoulders and put back one of the two menus she had picked up.

I took a look around to get a first impression of the room—upscale, with white tablecloths and cloth napkins, but not overdone for a mid-range meatery. And then I saw him.

At a table on the back wall sat my old buddy Detective Joe with a woman I expected was his wife. Of course he was looking right back at me. I was sure he always watched the door—probably a cop thing. I was busted quicker than a lobster claw at a clam bake.

I followed the hostess to my booth, thanked her, and then slunk to the detective's table—my head hung low like that of a puppy caught on the dining room table next to a licked-clean dinner plate.

"This is how you don't leave town?" was the detective's opening volley.

"I've had this restaurant review on my calendar for weeks. I didn't want to cancel at the last minute. And though it might not be the same town, it's still in the same county." I was hoping to get off on a technicality.

"You don't seem to realize that you're a suspect in a murder investigation, showing up in town right before a dead body turns up."

I was still convinced that I didn't do it.

"Who's your friend, dear?" the woman with Joe asked.

"He's not my friend. He could be a cold-blooded killer."

"I'm Murph, Mrs.…um…Detective." I couldn't for the life of me remember the stack of letters from the nameplate. "Your husband gives me far too much credit."

I put out my hand to shake hers, but Joe slapped it away.

"It's so nice to meet someone Joe works with," she offered graciously.

"Thank you." I turned to Joe, "Speaking of work, I understand that there's a business partner in the Rusty Pig."

"I know."

"I'm sure you do." And I meant it—the guy seemed pretty sharp. "I was wondering what you knew about him," I prodded.

"I know a lot of things about him—things you don't need to know."

"Oh, honey, help your partner out," his wife interjected.

"He's not my partner. He's a suspect." He turned back to me, "Look, if I give you something, will you stay in town and out of my way?"

"I, um..."

"Out with it."

"I have a lunch review tomorrow at Obsidian."

Pro tip: When a place is very expensive for dinner, like Obsidian, go for lunch instead. While it still won't be cheap, you can get the same quality food and service at a much better price.

"What?" he said loudly. "Obsidian is 50 miles from here. What don't you understand about 'Don't leave town?'"

"I know, but I'll come back right after lunch."

"At least you'll be out of my hair for a while. Be sure to ask for Laurel while you're there. She's the bartender."

"She's our daughter," his wife added.

Great. He would have eyes on me there, too.

If nothing else, I could try to get some food tips from the detective and his wife. "Do you come here often? What do you recommend?"

"I recommend you skip dessert." He reached out and flipped the overworked button barely holding my jacket closed."

Mrs. Detective said, "The scallop appetizer is my favorite."

Seafood at a steak place—not my first choice. Still, it would be nice to have something to erase my memory of the last, fraudulent scallop I ate. I thanked the nice lady and slipped away to the refuge of my private booth.

Nuts—I remembered the detective said he would tell me about Matt's business partner.

Before I could make the terrible decision to return to their table, the waiter arrived.

"What can I bring you?" he asked.

I definitely needed something to relax me. Without looking at the wine list, I took a chance. "I'll have the house red."

"The house red?"

"Wine," I added.

"Oh, of course." He turned.

"And a glass of water." But it was too late—he was gone.

The evening proceeded slowly from there. I was able to order the water, then he was gone again. Next, I ordered the scallop appetizer. As the waiter disappeared, I watched Mr. and Mrs. Detective get up and leave. She gave me a little wave on her way out.

My scallop arrived, lonely on its plate. It looked very familiar. I asked the waiter to wait while I cut into it and tasted. *As I suspected.*

"Who's your fishmonger?" I asked.

"My what?"

I rephrased, "Where do you get your seafood from?"

"Just a minute." He wandered off.

In less than a minute, a very well-fed man in a chef's hat stood at my booth. "You have a problem with your meal?"

"Not a problem, per se. I was asking where you get your seafood."

"You're that restaurant critic, aren't you?"

"Yes. We might have spoken on the phone. I'm Murph." I didn't offer my hand as I was growing fearful of rejection.

"Was that tonight you were coming?"

"Yup. Here I am."

"Hmph. How's your meal so far? I see you ordered the scallop."

He could also see I had only taken one nibble off of it. "It was recommended. Where does it come from?"

"I'll send out their card."

And with that, he was gone. No talk about any specials or even a signature dish that I shouldn't miss. The waiter reappeared and handed me a business card. I read "Amalgamated Seafood" then pocketed it next to the stroopwafel.

"Thank you. I'm ready to order."

"Okay," he said, and walked off again.

Service didn't seem to be their strong suit. The food, so far, didn't seem to be either. My wine, on the other hand, was the only thing getting me through the evening. The waiter returned promptly this time, tightly squeezing a pad and pencil.

"I'll have the 16-ounce NY strip, medium rare." Seemed like a good plan at a place named "Steak." I had the feeling he was about to turn and run so I quickly added, "And the baked potato with only butter. What's the vegetable of the day?"

Oh, nuts, I blew it.

He took off for the kitchen. At least I had plenty of time to shoot some video and work on my review.

The steak, as it turned out, was actually quite good—cooked to a perfect medium rare and well-seasoned. The broccoli was just the way I liked it, almost raw, and the baked potato was a potato that was baked—nothing special, but fine.

The bill showed up before any suggestion for dessert. Maybe the detective had had a word with my waiter. I paid cash—I was afraid that if I put out a credit card, I might have been having breakfast there.

I didn't want dessert at Steak, anyway. I had a chocolate orange croissant waiting for me at The Apple, if there were any left.

Chapter Ten

The Apple Bakery was hopping. I hoped that Detective Joe was not among the giddy crowd. If I didn't know better, I'd have thought the place had an open bar.

I made my way to the bakery case and spotted her—the last chocolate orange croissant. Now if only I could get the server's attention before it was too late. It was finally my turn and she was mine.

Granted, this croissant was not quite as good as the warm one I'd had earlier in the day. But it was still worth the claustrophobic feel of this place. And all of the hootin' and hollerin'— what was this game they were playing?

Two tables in the middle of the room had four and five players, respectively, holding cards. There were also people playing at the long bar and lots of people watching, even from out on the sidewalk through the front window.

I pressed close to the four-top and stood trying to figure out the card game's rules. I asked the man next to me, who was also watching, what this was all about.

"You ain't never played All or Nothing before?"

"I don't think so." I wasn't much of a gamer. I found it got in the way of eating.

"It's simple. To win you need to take all of the tricks, or none of the tricks—All or Nothing, get it?

Well, no.

The man then spent the longest time telling me about the black and white suits and the flippers until I was totally confused and wished the place had an open bar. I finally excused myself and went to the counter to see if I could get a cup of coffee.

"I'm sorry, we're tapped," said the server.

While I was sure I didn't need the caffeine that late at night, I asked, "Is there a Starbucks or something nearby?"

"No, not yet. There's talk of Starbucks trying to buy a place in town to build a store."

"Are you worried what that might mean to The Apple?" I did enjoy a Starbucks pumpkin spice latte in season, but I didn't like what often happened to the small coffee houses near their countless locations.

"Nah, we're not worried. How was your croissant?"

Better than Starbucks, I had to agree.

It was late. I suddenly felt very tired, remembering I didn't get all that much sleep after the long drive into town last night. I headed for the Open Arms.

Chapter Eleven

The next morning, I took an invigorating walk around town and shot some B-roll to use when I put together my video for the blog.

I found a nice perch in a park and FaceTimed the number Matt had given me for his business partner, Hampton Collins. I soon saw the man's smiling face on my phone screen.

"Good morning, Mr. Collins. I'm Murph Murphy. I would like to speak with you about your business."

"I have many businesses. Is there one in particular, or shall we simply start at the top of the list?"

He looked a bit imperious on my little screen. I replied, "The Rusty Pig."

"Oh, yes. You're the restaurant critic. Matt told me you were kind enough to offer us a review. What did you think?"

"The smoker was out of service when I got there so I've only been able to enjoy the lemonade, so far."

"You say there was a problem with the smoker? I'll have to look into that. Can't let my investments go too long without checking up on them. Thank you for making me aware of the situation." His voice was oily and dismissive.

I wouldn't be dismissed. "I thought I saw you there as the smoker was being removed by the police."

"Did you? Perhaps you were mistaken. I don't get that way often, though Matt's food is fabulous. I'm sorry you missed it. Now, if there's nothing else."

The man could talk in more circles than a plate of onion rings.

"Well, yes. There's the reason I called. I took a look at the books for the Rusty Pig and thought you might be able to help me sort out some anomalies."

"Those are confidential. How would you happen across them?"

"Matt took me through them on the computer."

"I didn't think he had those skills. It looks like I'll have to change the password."

I pushed on. "I'm sure you're aware that Matt owns the building and land that comprises the Rusty Pig."

"I am well aware of that."

"Then can you explain why there's an expense for rent every month?"

"Perhaps it's for equipment rental. Maybe you don't understand the accounting for a restaurant."

"Believe me, Mr. Collins, I've done my time stewing in restaurant books. There are other discrepancies as well. Would you be willing to sit down and go over them with me?"

"I would, but I'm just not that familiar with all the specifics of my many businesses. I will find whoever in my office handles that and get it all squared away. Thank you for bringing it to my attention. Goodbye, Mr. Murphy."

And with that, my screen was blank. He had told me almost nothing, but maybe that said everything. He was certainly slick. And he had earned his spot on my suspect list. I was sure that the face on my phone was the same one I saw at the Pig the previous morning.

Ham and Matt effectively had the same incentive to see the restaurant closed, depending on which of them had doctored the books and hidden the embezzled funds. But that still didn't explain the murder and the timing of it all.

I was glad for the long drive to lunch to clear my head. I needed to be sharp for my sampling of Obsidian.

Chapter Twelve

I took a stool at Obsidian's bar and looked across to its tendress.

"What can I get you?" She had her line down perfectly.

"Information," I responded, trying to sound as much like a private dick as I could.

She laughed and said, "You sound like my dad."

As I thought. "Laurel?"

"Yes. Have we met?"

"No, I'm Murph. Your father told me to check in with you. Apparently I'm his main suspect in a murder case."

"And he sent you to me? Am I supposed to get you liquored up and see if you'll talk?"

"Perhaps—though I talk plenty, even without booze."

Just then I felt a presence.

"There you are," Kimber said.

How did she find me?

That needed to be said out loud. "How did you find me?"

"It wasn't hard. You publish where you're headed on your blog."

"I don't list my exact schedule."

"A few phone calls—no big deal."

Stalker it was. I supposed I should have been more careful than to lay out my plans for the world to see. I remembered something about keeping your friends close and your enemies closer. "I was about to have lunch. Care to join me?"

"I would be happy to be your date," Kimber bubbled.

Laurel took us to a nearby table and pointed out the wine list.

"A bit too early in the day for me—just water, please," I said.

Kimber piped right up, "I'll have something. It's never too early for me."

Can't say I was surprised. But I was already starting to add up the potential cost of this meal in my head. While it was less expensive at lunch, I hadn't counted on paying for two meals. Plus, Kimber ordered the most expensive wine they sold by the glass. Don't get me wrong—I was actually lucky enough to be able to make a living as a food critic and blogger, supported by ads and sponsors, but I wasn't exactly rolling in dough. Scarily, she seemed to read my mind.

"Don't worry, I'm buying our lunch. It will be a real thrill when I see it on your blog. Any chance you could put my picture on there?"

I had lost control of this whole thing some time ago. "Sure. I'll need you to sign a release."

Mercifully, the waiter appeared. "Mr. Murphy, I'm Josh. It will be my pleasure to serve you and your guest."

Kimber interrupted, "By the way, I'm sorry I missed you at breakfast."

The waiter must have thought she was talking to him. "Oh, we're not open for breakfast during the week. We do offer a lavish brunch on Sunday."

Yes, she caught me. I didn't have breakfast at the Open Arms. I made yet another appearance at The Apple. Their fresh-daily bagels—water boiled and everything—made for a great egg sandwich. As a footnote, the baker acted as if she had never seen me before.

Something clicked in the deep recesses of what passed for my mind—the Rusty Pig wasn't open for breakfast. Why was the waitress there that early in the morning? Surely her shift wouldn't start till closer to lunch. More fodder for my growing suspect list.

The Obsidian lunch menu went far beyond burgers. Kimber ordered a duck appetizer and half a roasted chicken with fries. I ordered a beet salad and beef bourguignon. Of course I had to review a dessert—it was part of the job—a hazelnut torte was ordered as well.

I spent the next hour tasting delectable food and learning everything Kimber. She was a foodie, of course. She was divorced, but didn't seem interested in me in that way—but remember, I couldn't read women. She got a lot— "a really lot," she said—of money in her divorce, which was great for me—a stalker with unlimited resources. And she would be headed home tomorrow—so there was some good news.

I would have liked to have been headed home, too, but I imagined I still wasn't allowed to leave the town I wasn't in at that moment. I wondered if Kimber should be added to my suspect list. She was a visitor, like me. Perhaps she didn't divorce her husband as much as murder him. I bet the detective already knew all about her. Still, it couldn't hurt to ask a few pointed questions.

"How long did you say you've been divorced?"

"Long enough, but you're not my type."

I didn't think she was interested in me, but it still hurt to hear it out loud.

The food at Obsidian was excellent, as expected. The dense chew of the sweet, vinegary, sliced beets contrasted nicely with the crunchy greens. Kimber's chicken was simply-seasoned with rosemary and garlic, and not dry in the least. Pictures and notes were taken—by both me and Kimber—you would have to check with her about the duck carpaccio as she raced through it before I could get a bite. I was beginning to think her plan might be to start her own food blog and outshine mine.

Every now and then, the large purse on the floor next to Kimber wriggled and she would reach down and drop a scrap of food from her plate into it. I was sure it was a health code violation, but as long as no one else noticed, I wasn't going to spill the beans.

Soon, but not soon enough, it was over. Kimber paid the bill, as she said she would, then disappeared through the front door with nary a last word. I left a generous tip and went to sit at the bar for a few minutes.

"What was that all about?" Laurel asked.

"All I can say is that if something happens to me, it was her. Tell your father I said 'Hello.'"

"You'll probably see him before I do, being his number-one suspect. You know he always gets his man," she said with a smile.

I was sure he did. "By the way, do you know where Amalgamated Seafood is?"

She gave me directions and, with a tip to her of my invisible hat, I hit the Men's room—it was a long drive—then I left.

Chapter Thirteen

Amalgamated Seafood was on the way back to town—that's the story I would tell Detective Joe, if pressed. I hadn't forgotten about the fake scallops and the fishy fish, much as I might have liked.

I pulled up to the large warehouse, surrounded by a tall fence. I stopped one of the workers outside and asked to see the warehouse manager.

"He hasn't been in for a couple of days," was the gruff response.

"Do you know when he'll be back?"

"I don't keep his calendar." He started to walk away.

"Mind if I look around?"

"Ain't nobody gonna stop you." Then I was alone.

I opened the front door and stepped into a small lobby. Off to one side was a steel door I expected went into the warehouse. I didn't see anyone through the large glass window of the office in the back, so I went in and nosed around.

The sign on the desk read "Ducky Holt"—probably the manager who was out. I poked at the papers on the desk. I didn't see what I was looking for.

Next stop—the filing cabinet. I found the file folder with the most recent manifests. There were lots of incoming shipments for cheaper fish like tilapia and catfish, and outgoing orders for more expensive fish like Chilean sea bass. One might have expected product going out would match product coming in—not so here.

I left the office and opened the steel door to the warehouse. There were forklifts moving pallets of goods onto and off of trucks. Nobody was paying attention to me, so I took a stroll to find the cooler where all the seafood was stored.

Inside the walk-in freezer was a worktable with an assortment of knives and a cookie cutter that looked to be the same size and shape as the "scallops" I had been served. I wondered what cheap substitute they were using.

There was a bump at the door—I decided my unauthorized visit was over. The thought of getting locked in a freezer, either accidentally or on purpose, left me cold. I went to sit with Irma and warm up a bit before heading back to town.

So, Ducky hadn't been around? Maybe he was hiding out, having recently killed someone—somcone who figured out what was happening here. My suspect list was getting long.

I decided to go find out if the detective knew about Ducky, or if there was any new information in the case he had neglected to pass along.

Chapter Fourteen

The desk officer at the police station took me back to the detective right away.

"C'mon in, Mr. Murphy, and have a seat. I was wondering when I would see you next. How was Obsidian?"

"Worth the drive. Your daughter says, 'Hello.'"

Before we could get past the small talk and down to the meat of the matter, in walked the ME. At least the door was open this time.

"Oh, I'm interrupting again," he said.

The detective said, "It's okay, Lou. Mr. Murphy might as well hear what you have to say. He seems to find out sooner or later anyway."

"The DNA came back on the body in the smoker. His name is Donald Holt."

I couldn't stop myself, "Ducky Holt?"

"So you admit you know the victim," the detective said.

Why couldn't I keep my mouth shut?

"I don't know him personally. I only know he's the manager at Amalgamated Seafood, and nobody's seen him for a few days."

"And how do you know this?"

"It's your wife's fault, actually. She suggested I try the scallop."

"What are you talking about?"

"The scallops at Steak, where we enjoyed that awkward meal together, and the Seaside Bistro here in town weren't sea scallops at all. They were made from something cheaper, possibly shark. I went to investigate and found that Ducky worked at the warehouse they came from but hadn't been seen for a couple of days."

"What does this have to do with anything?"

"I'm not really sure. Maybe Ducky was killed for selling fake food."

"But you seem to be the only one who knows about the fake food."

I was really good at making myself look guilty. I'd better point the finger at someone else in a hurry.

"Other people might have known about it, too. What about Kimberly Wilson? She's into food and she's a visitor, just like me."

"Yes, I'm aware that Mrs. Wilson is staying at the Open Arms with you."

"She's not staying with me!" I protested too much, but it was out there now.

The detective followed up, "Why would she kill Mr. Holt?"

"She wasn't married to him by any chance, was she?"

"She was not."

In that case, I had nothin'. I closed my eyes and sat quietly, waiting to hear the click of handcuffs.

"You finally ready to stay out of this case and my way?" the detective asked.

Unfortunately, I wasn't. I wanted to talk to Katie again.

Chapter Fifteen

Katie appeared to be in better spirits. She answered the front door herself. I didn't see her mother anywhere.

"Hello, Mr. Murphy."

"Please, call me Murph."

"Would you like something to drink?" she asked.

I followed her to the kitchen. Before I could order, there was a short knock on the front door, and I heard it open.

Katie turned to the living room. I hung back in the kitchen and peered out, hiding like a piece of chicken in a bowl of matzo ball soup.

"Jeremy? You're alive!" She ran to her boyfriend and wrapped her arms around him. "I can't believe it!" She reached up to kiss him.

He shrugged her off. "Of course I'm alive. Why wouldn't I be?"

"Something terrible happened at the Rusty Pig," she said.

"That place, again? I told you to quit that stupid job. I make more than enough money to take care of both of us."

"We've already had this fight. I like my job, and I don't want you taking care of me."

I stepped out of the shadows before things could escalate.

Jeremy looked at me, then back at Katie. "Who is he?" he demanded.

"I'm Murphy. Why don't you chill a bit, and we can all chat."

"I don't need to chill. I need a beer. Get me one, would you, babe?"

"Aren't you still working today?" she asked.

"No, I can't get ahold of Ducky, so I guess I'm off for the rest of the day."

I asked, "You know Ducky Holt?"

"He's my boss. What's it to you? Katie, who is this guy?"

"He's a friend. He just dropped by."

I stepped in as I could feel another fight starting. "I came to talk to Katie about Ducky. You might want to have a seat, Jeremy."

"I don't take orders from you."

"Suit yourself. Can I ask where your hat is? I hear you never go anywhere without it."

"My hat? Why do you care? I lost it. I don't know where. What's going on?"

"Ducky Holt was found dead at the Rusty Pig—by Katie."

"Ducky? Dead? Katie?" Jeremy acted like this was the first he had heard of it.

She put her hands on her hips. "Yes. I found him—along with your hat."

I was pleased she didn't offer too many additional details, as I wanted to see if Jeremy might let something slip.

"I've got to talk to Mr. Collins," he said.

"Hampton Collins? You know him, too?" I asked.

"He owns Amalgamated Seafood."

So, the stock thickens.

Katie still wanted answers. "What about your hat, Jeremy?"

"I don't know. I said I lost it."

This wasn't getting us anywhere. "I think it's time we go see the police detective. He's been looking for you. C'mon, I'll drive." I ushered the two of them out the front door.

Jeremy said, "I'll be right there," and went to his truck as I headed for Irma.

Katie shouted, "Shotgun!"

I called over my shoulder, "Yes, you can sit up front."

"No," she said and pointed. "He has a shotgun."

Of course he did. I pushed Katie behind me, out of the line of fire.

"Back into the house." Jeremy herded us back through the front door, waving the muzzle of the weapon. "I don't know what you think I did, but I'm not going to jail again. Stay here and you won't get hurt. I've got to find Mr. Collins."

I heard his truck start and burn rubber down the street. I had no intention of chasing him. I did, however, have a phone and the detective's number.

After I left a short message, I asked Katie, "Did you know Jeremy had been in jail?"

"No. I guess he's not the good guy I thought he was. Still, I'm glad it wasn't him I ate."

It sounded like she was well on her way to recovery.

"I've wanted to ask you—why were you at the Pig so early yesterday morning?"

"I needed to talk to Matt. I waited for him out by the smoker while he was in the kitchen getting the food ready. That's when I noticed the sweet smell coming from the smoker."

I did not want to revisit that part of her morning. "Was there something in particular you wanted to talk to Matt about?"

She hesitated. "I had that fight with Jeremy at work in front of him the day before. It was a little embarrassing, and I wanted to make sure Matt was okay with me."

I decided to put it out there. "So how come you're not with Matt? He seems like a genuinely nice guy."

"He doesn't think of me like that. He's my boss and we're just friends."

"Are you sure?" She seemed to read men as well as I read women.

"Do you know something I don't?"

"I know how to make beer-can chicken, do you?" I didn't want to overstep my bounds—at least not any further.

I hugged Katie goodbye and peeked out the door to ensure Jeremy was gone. I might not be brave, but I also wasn't stupid. I took the short walk to the Pig.

Chapter Sixteen

The front door of the Rusty Pig was open so I made myself at home at one of the four-tops. I figured Matt was around somewhere and when he turned up, he might offer me more of that lemonade.

While I waited, I reviewed my long suspect list. My top pick was Sam, the owner of the Seaside Bistro, if for no other reason than the meal he served me was a crime. His motive could have been to get rid of the competition.

Next on the list was Katie—I hoped it wasn't her. But she could have had motive, either killing her boyfriend's boss for reasons unknown to me or helping Jeremy do it. But why take down Matt at the same time? She seemed to like him and her job.

Which brought us to Matt. If he was the mastermind behind the murder, it could have been for financial reasons—possibly to cover up money laundering. I wasn't well-connected enough in this town to follow the money. The Pig got deliveries from Amalgamated Seafood, so he might have known and had a beef with Ducky. The guy was selling counterfeit food. And setting up Jeremy, a guy he clearly wasn't a fan of, would have been a nice touch.

And, of course, there was Ham, and I didn't mean the poor relative of delicious bacon. He was Ducky's boss, and I was sure I saw him around the crime scene, even though he denied it. I wouldn't put embezzling from the Pig past him. And who knows what else fishy was happening at Amalgamated Seafood, besides the scallops.

Then there was Jeremy. Everything pointed to him. He worked for Ducky. He wanted Katie out of her job at the Pig, and getting it shut down would make that happen. His hat was even at the crime scene. And he bolted rather than talk to the cops. But it seemed a little too pat. Plus, it looked like he had no idea Ducky was dead.

Who was I missing? Kimber? No, I definitely did not miss Kimber. There was nothing connecting her to the crime other than she was in town at the time, like all the other townsfolk, and me. She was off the list.

I heard the back door open. I was thirsty and ready to talk to Matt. But it wasn't Matt.

"Mr. Collins. What are you doing here?"

"I'm part owner of this business. Why are you here? The place is closed." He hastily stuffed a wad of clothing behind the counter.

"I was hoping to talk to Matt, but maybe you and I can chat instead." I hadn't had much quality time with Ham, and it was as good a time as any to see what he knew about the many suspects that were still on my list.

"As you see, Matt isn't here, and I don't have time for you. I need to gather some of my property and get going. You should move along." He started disconnecting wires from the computer.

"It looks like you think the Rusty Pig is toast."

"It no longer makes financial sense, and with the death of that poor man, I have made the decision to close it."

"Doesn't your partner have a say in the decision?"

"Matt has no money and therefore no say. Good day, Mr. Murphy."

I had no intention of leaving. "About that—why doesn't Matt have any money? The Pig was pulling in plenty and he didn't seem to get his share. Perhaps someone else's hand was in the till? In any case, I have some money I want to use to stake Matt. I'll give him a call and we can all sit down and talk about it."

Ham stopped dissecting the computer. "Mr. Murphy, why do you insist on making this difficult for me?"

"Well, in addition to your not treating Matt fairly, I have eaten some of the phony food your business, Adulterated Seafood, sells."

"It's Amalgamated Seafood, and we have never had a complaint about any of its products."

"Put me down for two complaints. Did your employee, Ducky, have any complaints?"

"It's really too bad what happened to him—being cooked like that must be a terrible way to go."

Ham had jumped to the top of my suspect list. "How did you know it was Ducky in the smoker?"

"Oh. I saw him in there before the police hauled it away yesterday."

"But you insisted you weren't here then. Tell me what really happened."

Ham sat down in the chair across from me.

"If you must know, Ducky was always asking for more money to keep his big mouth shut about the work he did for me."

"So he had to go," I prompted.

"It was easy enough to get him drunk and load him into the smoker. I knew that his being found here would be the end of the Rusty Pig."

I still didn't understand. "You could have kept embezzling and stringing Ducky along. Why kill him now?"

"Damned Starbucks. Of all the property I own in this town, they want the one piece Matt owns—the Rusty Pig. I knew he wouldn't sell it to me so that I could turn around and sell it to Starbucks at a nice profit, so it was time for Ducky to go. Two birds, one stone. Now that this place is out of business, I will make Matt a token offer to take the burden off his hands. I'm helpful like that."

Money—it always came down to money—when it wasn't love, anyway.

"Are you helpful enough to turn yourself in?" I sensed that I may have gotten in over my head.

Ham reached into his jacket pocket. For the second time that day, there was a gun pointed my way.

Chapter Seventeen

I slid my chair back. "I really should move along. What's a little embezzling and murder between friends?"

"Spare me." Ham slid his finger to the trigger. "We both know you're not going to let this go."

"A smart guy like you wouldn't shoot me with your own gun." I needed to buy some time to come up with a plan.

"You're right. I'm sure we can find a more creative way for you to off yourself, despondent over what you did to Ducky. Perhaps your culinary prowess might come in handy. How would you choose to die that would make a fitting finale for that tripe you publish?"

Now there was an interesting question I had never considered. If my life was food, what should my death look like? "How about by eating too many pastries? I already have a pretty good head start."

"That might take too long," he countered.

I saw him eyeing the fryer. I couldn't think of any good that could come of that.

He stood and waved the pistol at me. "Let's see if the oven is gas. Get up."

I looked past him at the cable dangling from the computer. What could I use to get out of being murdered? As I started to stand, I heard a little crinkling sound from my jacket and came up with a plan. I jumped up from my seat clumsily, knocking the chair backward as I did. I turned to pick it up.

"Leave it," Ham commanded.

While my back was to him, I reached into my coat pocket. As I turned back, I launched a stroopwafel into his face. It wasn't much, but it was enough to startle him and give me time to grab for his gun. While I couldn't get him to let go of it, I was able to keep the business end pointed away from me as we wrestled across the table.

Just then the detective entered the front door, his ubiquitous gun drawn this time. "That's enough. Drop your weapon, Mr. Collins. You're under arrest for the murder of Donald Holt."

Ham released the gun to me and I laid it on the table, out of his reach.

After an officer handcuffed Ham and led him away, I headed to the fridge and found the lemonade. I poured two glasses and offered the detective one.

"How did you find me?" I asked.

"I went to see Miss Miller after I got your message about Jenks, and she said she saw you head this way. I sat on the front porch listening to you get Mr. Collins to confess—nicely done."

"Thank you. Before I forget, I believe you'll find Ducky's clothes behind the counter. Can I leave town now?"

"I haven't been able to stop you so far. But you'll need to come by the station and give a statement." He took a sip from his glass and smiled. "Can I get this lemonade to go?"

I poured both our drinks into paper cups.

As we walked out, I heard a crunch from the floor. My poor stroopwafel—he died a hero.

Chapter *Fin*

The email subject line read "Grand Reopening of
the Rusty Pig." That was all I needed to know.

"C'mon, Irma, we're going back to the
Pig."

It was short notice for a long drive, but I
always had a change of clothes in the car—de
rigueur for a sloppy chowhound.

I joined a group of enthusiastic eaters at
one of the picnic tables out back of a newly
upgraded Rusty Pig and marveled at the variety
of smoked meats on my plate. I started with the
pulled pork. The spicy barbeque sauce danced on
my tongue.

Matt soon joined me. "I'm glad you made
it back, Mr. Murphy!"

"It's still Murph. I like the new digs. Nice
that you kept the old sign."

"With all the money from selling the old place to Starbucks, we could afford to move the Pig to a new, bigger home."

Katie walked up and leaned into Matt. He slipped his arm around her waist.

Matt grinned. "Plus, Katie is taking business classes at the community college, so we should be able to keep this one going."

"That is excellent. Tell me, where did you find a smoker just like Old Betsy?"

"That is Old Betsy."

The partially-chewed rib bone I was holding clattered to the plate.

Murph's Salmon

A quick and easy-to-prepare dinner.

Place a thick filet of Atlantic salmon, skin side down, onto a sheet pan. Salt it liberally while waiting for the oven to preheat to 350 degrees. Sprinkle with thyme and pepper to taste.

Cut a head of broccoli into bite-sized pieces and spritz with olive oil. Sprinkle lightly with turmeric and season with salt. Arrange in a single layer on the sheet pan next to the salmon.

Bake (or grill, covered) about 20 minutes. The broccoli will come out nicely roasted when the salmon is done. Serve with rice or save the calories for dessert.

Pro tips: Cover the sheet pan in aluminum foil or parchment paper for easier cleanup. Check the salmon carefully for any bones or scales that got past the fishmonger. Instead of thyme, sprinkle the salmon with tarragon, lemon pepper, garam masala, or another seasoning of your choice. Substitute asparagus or sliced squash for the broccoli. Leftover baked salmon with arugula and pesto on ciabatta makes an excellent sandwich.

Thank you for reading *Smoked: A Snack-Sized Mystery*. We hope you enjoyed the ride. Please leave a review on Amazon and / or Goodreads, and tell your friends.

Join Murph on all his culinary adventures:
Smoked: A Snack-Sized Mystery (1)
Cracked: A Snack-Sized Mystery (2)
Tossed: A Snack-Sized Mystery *Cruise* (3)
Squashed: A Snack-Sized Mystery (4)
Toasted: A Snack-Sized Mystery *Wedding* (5)

More at JmarsInk.com.

About the Author

Jeff Schmoyer tries to find humor in the crazy world around him. Several of his short plays have been produced, and his short stories have been published in the Pikes Peak Writers anthologies, *Journeys into Possibility* and *The Other Side of the Mountain*. He is the author of the **Snack-Sized Mystery** series starring food blogger Murph Murphy, including *Smoked*, *Cracked*, *Tossed*, *Squashed*, and *Toasted*. He is always up for a tasty meal and a friendly game of cards. Find more at JmarsInk.com.